10
TURKEYS
IN THE ROAD

BY Brenda Reeves Sturgis
ILLUSTRATED BY David Slonim

two lions

two lions

Text copyright © 2011 by Brenda Reeves Sturgis
Illustrations copyright © 2011 by David Slonim

All rights reserved
No part of this book may be reproduced, or stored in a retrieval system, or transmitted
in any form or by any means, electronic, mechanical, photocopying, recording, or otherwise,
without express written permission of the publisher.
Published by Two Lions, New York
www.apub.com
Amazon, the Amazon logo, and Two Lions are trademarks of Amazon.com, Inc., or its affiliates.
Library of Congress Cataloging-in-Publication Data
Reeves Sturgis, Brenda.
10 turkeys in the road / by Brenda Reeves Sturgis ; illustrated by David
Slonim.— 1st ed.
p. cm.
Summary: Ten turkeys performing circus acts block a country road, much to
the frustration of an angry farmer in a pick-up truck who tries to shoo them away.
ISBN-13: 9781542025379 (paperback) ISBN-10: 1542025370 (paperback)
[1. Stories in rhyme. 2. Turkeys—Fiction. 3. Circus—Fiction. 4. Counting.
5. Humorous stories.] I. Slonim, David, ill. II. Title. III. Title: Ten turkeys in the road.
PZ8.3.S9229Aai 2011
[E]—dc22
2010001232

The illustrations were rendered in acrylic.
Book design by Anahid Hamparian
Editor: Robin Benjamin

To all the turkeys in my life: Gary, Stacie, Seabren, Whitney, Seabren IV, Stephen and Courtney, Stephanie and Shaun, and the newest turkey babies. We have the greatest show on Earth! To Margery Cuyler and Robin Benjamin, the best ringmasters in this circus, and to Josh and Tracey Adams—thank you (no clowning around) for your hard work and friendship! Thank you also to my good friend Shari Dash Greenspan for everything!

—B.R.S.

To the Stellas,
who gave me my first unicycle

—D.S.

Ten turkeys blocked the road
one hot and hazy day.
A pickup screeched. A farmer beeped.
One turkey flew away.

Nine turkeys in the road
caused a long delay.
The farmer frowned and flashed his lights.
One turkey flew away.

Eight turkeys in the road,
each holding out a tray.
The farmer inched his truck ahead.
One turkey flew away.

Seven turkeys in the road
with cans of string to spray.
The farmer shook his fist and yelled.
One turkey flew away.

Six turkeys in the road
climbed high to swing and sway.
The farmer banged and clanged his tools.
One turkey flew away.

Five turkeys in the road
declared, "We're here to stay!"
The farmer threw his old straw hat.
One turkey flew away.

Four turkeys in the road
shared a big bouquet.
The farmer opened up his door.
One turkey flew away.

Three turkeys in the road
juggled bales of hay.
The farmer jumped and pulled his hair.
One turkey flew away.

TWO turkeys in the road
squawked, "Hip, hip, hooray!"
The farmer pounded on his hood.
One turkey flew away.

ONE turkey in the road
announced, "We've got to go!"

The turkeys snuck into the truck
and called, "Come see the show!"

One farmer in the road
hung his head and sighed.
A car drove up. The driver asked . . .
"Hey, pal, ya need a ride?"

The tired farmer huffed and puffed,
then squeezed into the car.
The driver squealed, "Away we go!
The circus isn't far!"

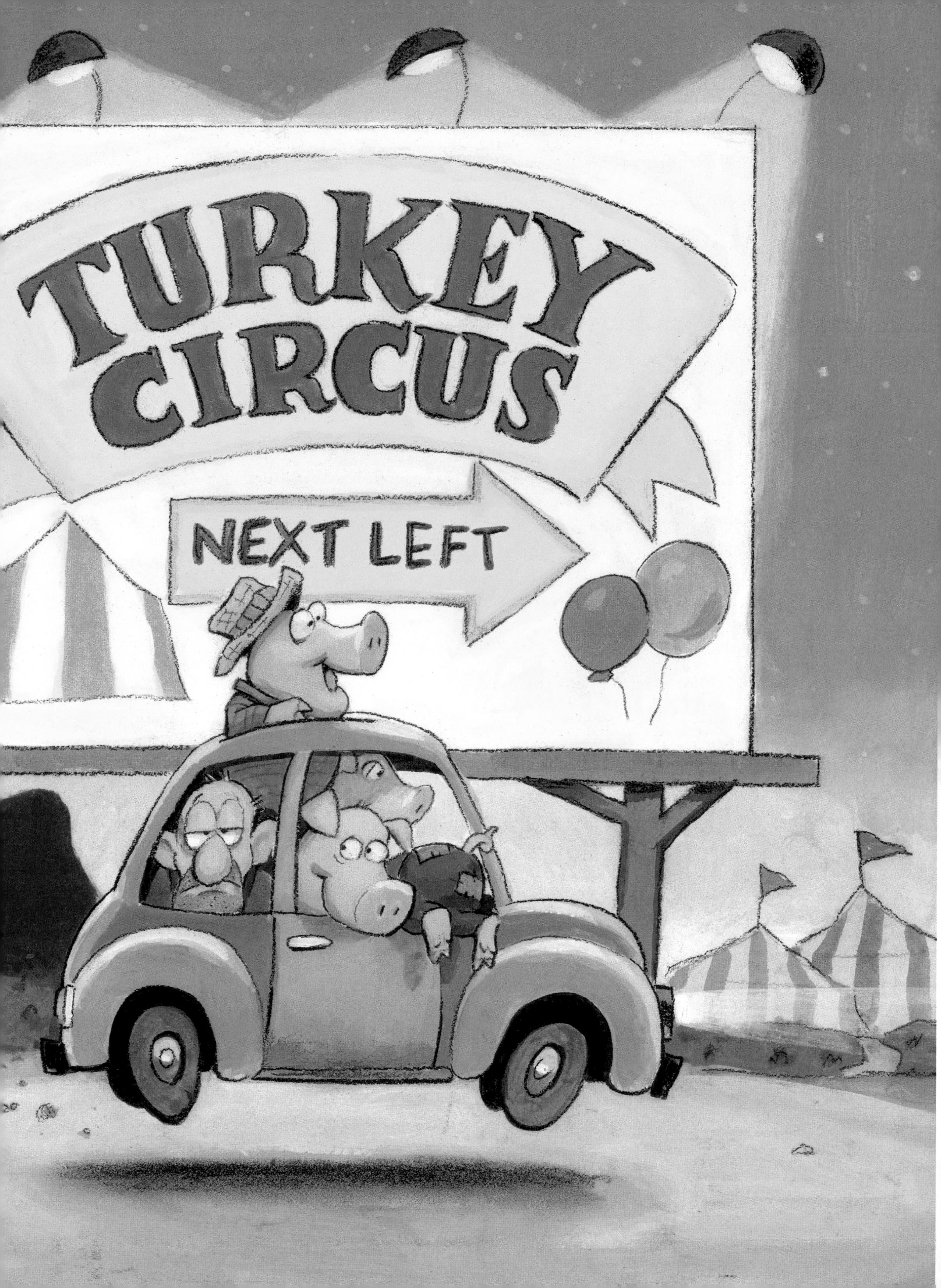
TURKEY CIRCUS
NEXT LEFT

THE END

Brenda Reeves Sturgis is an author who lives on a lovely little lake in Maine. She watches moose meander, listens to loons shrill, and enjoys troublemaking turkeys all from her front yard. Her life is *always* a circus, and she wouldn't want it any other way. Learn more at www.brendareevessturgis.com.

David Slonim received his BFA from the Rhode Island School of Design. He is the author-illustrator of several picture books, including *He Came with the Couch* and *Oh, Ducky!* He also illustrated *How to Teach a Slug to Read* by Susan Pearson, *Silly Tilly* by Eileen Spinelli, and *Bed Hog* by Georgette Noullet. He lives with his family in Indiana. Visit him at www.davidslonimpresents.com.